I Don't Want to Go Back to School

MARISABINA RUSSO

Greenwillow Books, New York

Gouache paints were used for the full-color art.
The text type is Helvetica Light.

Printed in Hong Kong by South China Printing
Company (1988) Ltd.

First Edition 10 9 8 7 6 5 4 3 2 1

Library of Congress Cataloging-in-Publication Data

Russo, Marisabina.
I don't want to go back to school / by Marisabina Russo.
p. cm.
Summary: Despite his older sister's dire warnings of all the terrible things that could go wrong on his first day in the second grade, Ben has a wonderful time.
ISBN 0-688-04601-0 (trade).
ISBN 0-688-04602-9 (lib. bdg.)
[1. Schools — Fiction.
2. Brothers and sisters — Fiction.]
I. Title. PZ7.R9192Iaac 1994 [E]—dc20
93-5479 CIP AC

For my son Benjamin,

and for his first-grade teacher,

Patricia Faigle

"Summer is almost over," said Mama. "Soon you will have to go back to school."

"Already?" said Ben. "Summer is so short! I don't want to go back to school."

"You're a big boy," said Mama. "You're going to be in second grade. You know what school is like."

"I wish I could stay home," said Ben.

The next day a letter arrived from Ben's school.
It said his new teacher would be Mr. Johnson.
"Mr. Johnson?" said Ben's big sister, Hannah.
"I remember the time he wouldn't let his class
go out for recess because..."
"Hannah!" said Daddy.

MAIL

"What if Mr. Johnson really is mean?" said Ben. "I don't want to go back to school."

"Remember the big yellow school bus?" said Mama. "You said you liked riding the bus to school."

"What if the driver misses my stop on the way home?" asked Ben.

"Or you fall asleep and miss your stop," said Hannah. "I did that once."

"Don't worry," said Mama. "I'll wait for your bus and make sure you get home."

"What if no one remembers me at school?" said Ben.

"All your friends will remember you," said Daddy.

"What if the teacher asks me a really hard question, and I don't know the answer?" said Ben.

"Yeah, like who was the first President to live in the White House?" said Hannah.

"I don't know," said Ben. "George Washington?"

"Wrong!" said Hannah. "It was John Adams."

"See, Mama?" said Ben. "That's why I don't want to go back to school."

Mama frowned at Hannah. Then she turned to Ben. "Don't worry. You're not supposed to know all the answers when you go to school."

When Mama woke Ben for the first day of school, he pretended he was still asleep.

"He's just faking," said Hannah. "I'll show you." She tickled his feet.

"Stop it," shrieked Ben.

"Come on, Ben. It's time to get up for school," said Mama.

"I don't want to go back to school. I feel sick," said Ben.

"You're not sick," said Hannah. "You're just a scaredy cat."

Kids Time

Ben got dressed and ate his breakfast.
He brushed his teeth and patted his dog
good-bye.

"Maybe we could send you instead of me,"
Ben said. "You could ride the bus and sit at
my desk and take a dog biscuit for snack...."

"Come on, Ben. It's time for your bus," said
Mama.

Hannah and Ben rode the same bus.
They sat together.
"Oh, I forgot to tell you Mr. Johnson keeps a giant tarantula in the closet," said Hannah. "When he gets mad, he lets it loose on your desk!"
"Be quiet, Hannah," said Ben.

When Ben got off the bus, he saw Isaac and Andy.
"Who's your teacher?" asked Isaac.
"Mr. Johnson," said Ben.
"We both got Miss Goldsmith," said Andy.
"Great," said Ben. "Now there's no one in my class."
"We'll see you at recess," said Andy.

Ben took a deep breath and walked into his classroom. There was Mr. Johnson. He was wearing a gray shirt and a tie with soccer balls on it.

"Hi, Ben," said a boy sitting in the front row. It was David.

"Okay, class," said Mr. Johnson. "Welcome to 2J. I want you all to meet my friend Millie." Mr. Johnson reached into a tank and pulled out a green scaly reptile. It was a lizard.

"If you look around, you will see we have a few other unusual classmates."

Ben and all the children looked around. They saw a turtle, a rabbit, and a snake. Ben wondered if there really was a tarantula in the closet.

Ff Gg Hh Ii Jj Kk Ll Mm
mmals
Reptiles
Can You

"We're going to start off the day with a game," said Mr. Johnson.
They played First Name Bingo. Ben won.
Then Mr. Johnson read them a book about a make-believe lizard family. Millie seemed to be listening, too. Mr. Johnson was a good reader. Ben liked the way he made all these funny voices for the different characters.

BY SAM

After snack Mr. Johnson pulled down the map of the world. He pointed to the United States and talked about places where lizards live.

"Ben, can you please show me where South America is?"

Ben felt his face grow warm. He walked up to the map. He didn't really know where to look.

"I'll give you a hint," said Mr. Johnson. "It's south of the United States."

Mr. Johnson didn't rush Ben. He let him run his finger down the map until he found South America.

"Good job," said Mr. Johnson.

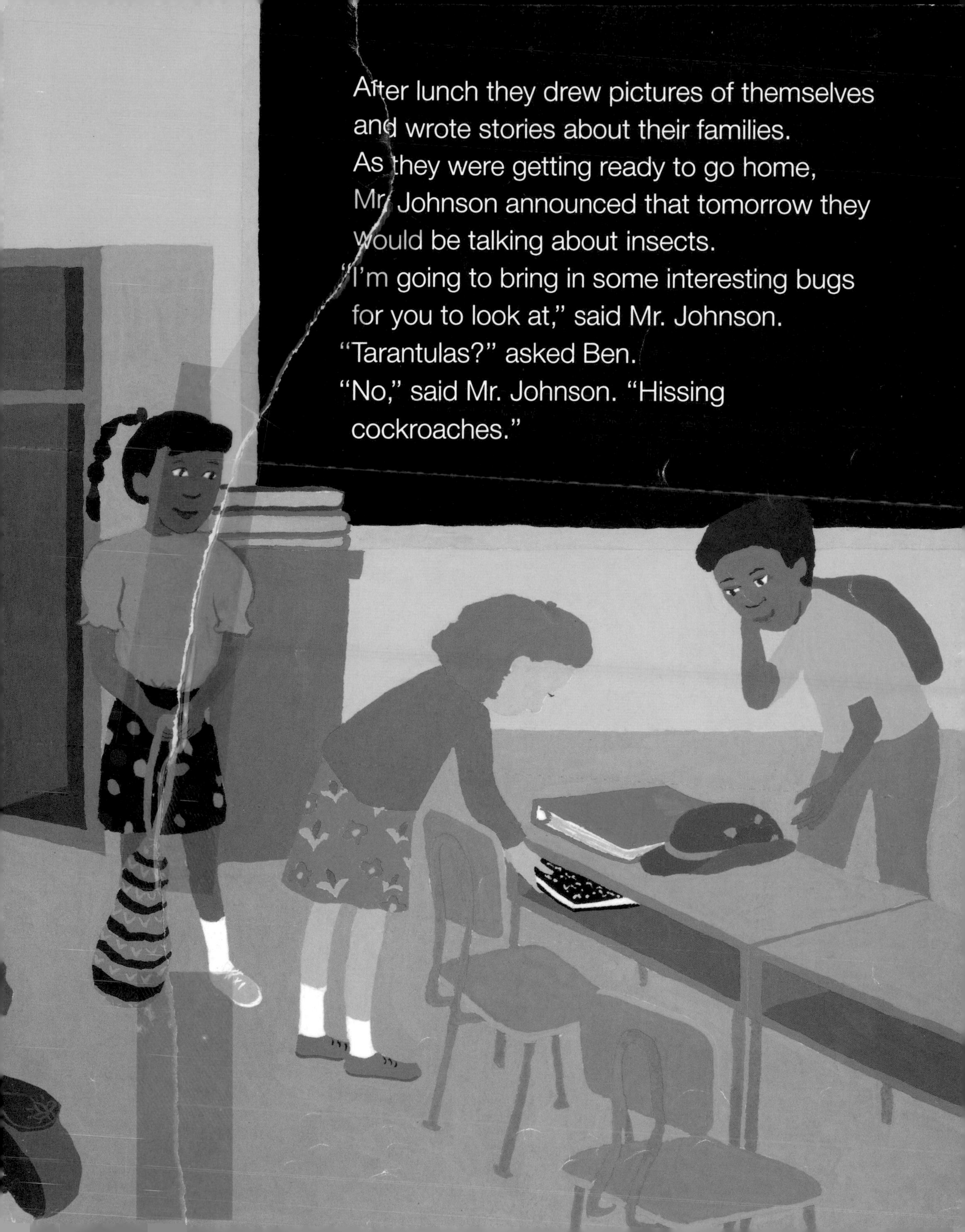

After lunch they drew pictures of themselves and wrote stories about their families. As they were getting ready to go home, Mr. Johnson announced that tomorrow they would be talking about insects.

"I'm going to bring in some interesting bugs for you to look at," said Mr. Johnson.

"Tarantulas?" asked Ben.

"No," said Mr. Johnson. "Hissing cockroaches."

When Ben got on the school bus, Hannah was already there.

"So, how was Mr. Johnson? Mean and rotten, huh?" said Hannah.

"No, he was nice," said Ben.

"What about his tarantulas? Weren't they hairy and big?" said Hannah.

"He doesn't have any tarantulas," said Ben.

"Did any of the kids remember you?" asked Hannah.

"Yes, everyone did," said Ben.

"Are you going to go back tomorrow?" asked Hannah.

"Of course," said Ben.

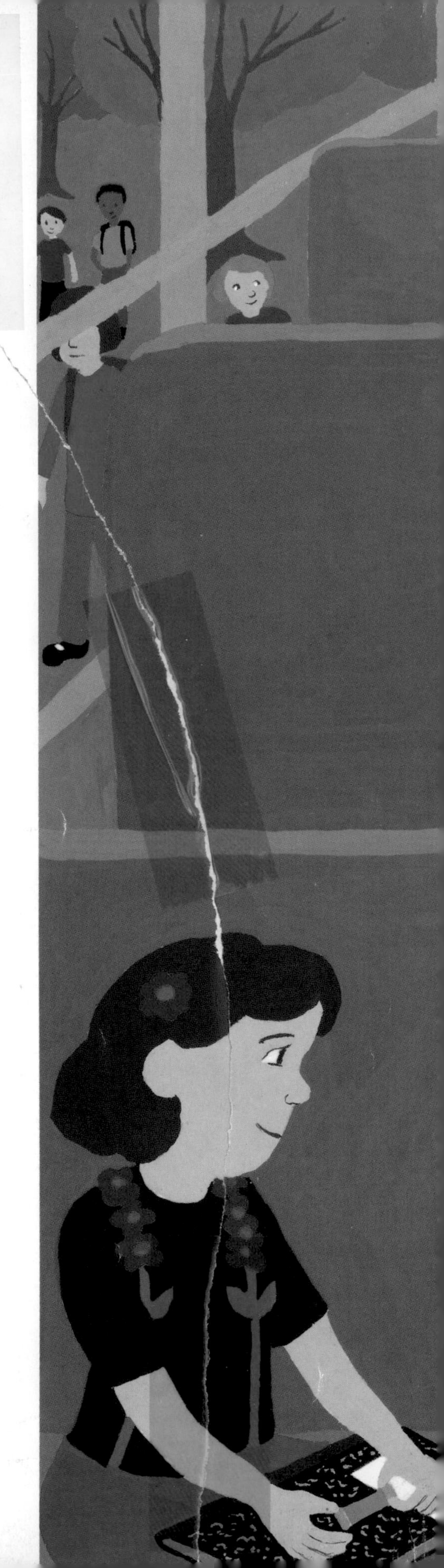

All the way home Ben looked out the window. He wanted to make sure he got off at the right stop. Then he saw Mama waiting on the corner.

"Come on, Hannah," said Ben. But Hannah didn't move. Ben had to wake her up, or she would have missed their stop.